E Pringle, Laurence
P Jesse builds a road

c.1   13.95

E
P
c.1   Pringle, Laurence
               Jesse builds a road.   Pictures by
           Leslie Holt Morrill.   Macmillan,
           1989.
               n.p.   col. illus.

           I. Title.

50373508   88-29297/13.95/1290

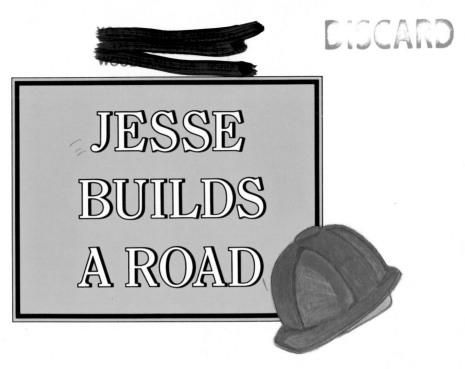

JESSE BUILDS A ROAD

By LAURENCE PRINGLE

Pictures by LESLIE HOLT MORRILL

Macmillan Publishing Company   New York

Collier Macmillan Publishers   London

Macmillan Publishing Company, 866 Third Avenue, New York, NY 10022
Collier Macmillan Canada, Inc.
Printed and bound in Singapore   First American Edition

10   9   8   7   6   5   4   3   2   1

The text of this book is set in 16 point Century Expanded.
The illustrations are rendered in watercolor and pencil.

Library of Congress Cataloging-in-Publication Data
Pringle, Laurence P.   Jesse builds a road/by Laurence Pringle; pictures by Leslie Holt Morrill.
—1st American ed.   p.   cm. Summary: Jesse's toys seem to come to life and shape a new
road as the little boy plays with his dump truck, bulldozer, and other road-building equipment.
ISBN 0-02-775311-5
[1. Road construction—Fiction. 2. Road machinery—Fiction. 3. Imagination—Fiction. 4. Play—Fiction.]
I. Morrill, Leslie H., ill. II. Title. PZ7.P93647Je 1989   [E]—dc19   88-29297 CIP AC

For Jesse

—L.P.

For Judith and Melissa

—L.H.M.

Jesse takes his dump truck out to the sandpile.
He brings his bulldozer and other equipment, too.
There is work to be done.

"Rowwrr, rowwrr."

Jesse makes the sounds of powerful engines.

"Rowwrr, rowwrr."

"Let's get to work,"
Jesse calls to his crew.

The bulldozer's steel tracks go "clank, clank, clank."
Its big blade pushes dirt and rocks to one side.

The front loader scoops up dirt,
then dumps it into a truck.

"Toot, toot, toot," warns its horn
as it backs up to get another scoopful.

The truck dumps dirt and rocks
at a low place in the new road.

"Bring another load," Jesse yells to the driver.

The tractor scraper
scrapes up a layer of earth,
then hauls it to a place
that needs to be filled in.

Something big blocks the path of the new road.
"We have to go around," Jesse says.

The bulldozer begins to clear the way.

"Hhhmmmm."
The grader moves
back and forth along the road,
making its surface smooth.

The road twists and turns up a hill,
then down the other side.

The machines halt at the edge of a gully.

"We need a bridge,"
Jesse tells the work crew.

A crane lifts girders
and sets them in place across the gully.

"Watch out! Here comes a flood," Jesse yells.

Water washes the bridge and part of the road away.

When the flood is over,
the machines build the bridge and the road again.
The air is filled with their sounds.

The machines come to a steep hillside.
A tunnel is needed, but the workers are tired.

"That's all for today," Jesse says.
"Work starts on the tunnel tomorrow."

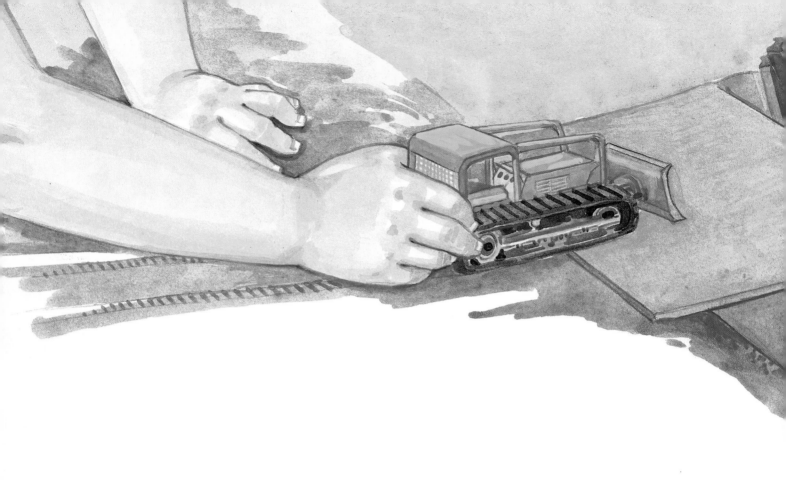

"Rowwrr, rowwrr."

One by one, Jesse parks the road-building machines.

"Rowwrr, rowwrr."
He shuts off their engines

and heads for home.